Inside *these* Walls

From Trauma to Triumph

AN ANTHOLOGY COMPILED BY
MICHELLE L. ANDERSON

Dedication

Inside these Walls, is for every heart that has been broken, every trauma experienced, and every secret kept.

May these pages be a reminder that you are not alone, your voice matters and that trauma does not have to win.

This book is dedicated to your hope, your forgiveness, your healing and rediscovering your voice.

Inside These Walls: From Trauma to Triumph

TABLE OF CONTENTS

Inside These Walls: From Trauma to Triumph

Trauma Did Not Win

Michelle L. Anderson

She does not love me.

I know she doesn't.

She did not even see the cuts on my arms.

Wait a minute, the teacher didn't see my cuts either!

Why isn't anyone paying attention?

I really don't want to kill myself, at least I don't think I do.

The cuts on my arms would have been deeper if I did, right?

I just want someone to see me, to hear me.

The cutting does not work, talking is not working.

I tried to tell my pastor, and he did not believe me.

He told me that it was just a dream.

How can I tell her if my pastor did not even believe me?

How can I tell her that her son touched me?

How can I tell her that two of her sons touched me?

Things were done to me that I did not think were possible.

I do not understand, why does he even like doing that to me?

Keeping my legs closed tight never helped.

Shaving hair that began to grow thinking he would not like

it anymore,

Never helped.

Going to bed fully dressed wearing layers,

Never helped.

It would not stop.

Nothing stopped it, not even the fact that her room was right

up under mine.

She could usually hear whenever I would get up at night to

use the bathroom.

Why doesn't she hear him when he walks into my room at

night?

Look at these pills, they say they cause drowsiness and

dizziness.

I do not know if they will kill me, but they will get her

attention, and she will see me then.

One, two, three pills down, a whole bottle to go.

Oh, my stomach, I woke up and ran to my bathroom as quickly as I could.

I could not stop throwing up, my stomach wouldn't stop turning.

My sister runs down the stairs yelling, "she's throwing up."

After laying on my bathroom floor in a ball, afraid to move an inch, for what seemed to be forever.

My grandmother finally took me to the doctor.

All I hear is, "you are so stupid."

"You better not be pregnant."

I cannot believe that out of all the things that came out of her mouth, never did she ask,

"Are you ok?"

I sat in the car silently.

She still didn't see me.

How would she ever hear me?

Have you ever felt like you weren't heard?

I wanted to scream at the top of my lungs, " he molested me over and over again." Since I could never be heard,

I resorted to cutting, taking pills, and just shutting down.

I silenced my pain.

What did you do when you wanted to be heard or seen?

If someone took the time to listen, what would you say?

Growing up I was taught, "What happens in this house, stays in this house." A saying that my generation knew all too well. What exactly was happening within the walls of the home, and why was it a secret? For so long, children have had to hold on to secrets that occur within the walls of the home, school, or church. They dare not speak about the pain within. One of the many secrets I had to keep growing up was child sexual abuse. The insert you read at the beginning of the chapter was a piece of writing I did about ten years ago, expressing the emotional pain sexual abuse caused me.

It grieves me to talk with my friends and learn of the sexual abuse they have also experienced. For some, sexual abuse was passed down from one generation to the next. I have heard stories of children, both boys and girls who were abused by a babysitter, cousin, neighbor or relative. 90% of children who are sexually abused know their abuser and 10% are sexually abused by strangers (Finklehor & Shuttuck,2012). These stats cause me to believe that the number one location for a child's sexual abuse is the home. How did I end up in a home with an abuser?

At a recent fundraiser, the women seated next to me asked about the types of jobs I've held. I began to list them. "Program manager, foster care worker, teacher, author." She followed up with, "wow, you must have great parents. I replied with, "not really, it was all God."

I began to share with her that I was in foster care and adopted, so my parents had no part in raising me. She looked at me as if she were sad for me. She tried to lighten the conversation by asking me what types of books I read. "Books on trauma," I exclaimed. I then began to show her my audio book library with Viola Davis's book, *Finding Me*, one of my favorite books. Despite the trauma she experienced as a child, she has been able to rise above it all.

It is interesting to me that I experienced various forms of trauma, yet I study it. You think I would stray far away from the topic. Instead, I seek more and more knowledge regarding it. If you noticed, I gave God the honor for me being where I am today. It is because of God and my experiences that I am writing this book and why my mission in life is to help heal and prevent childhood trauma.

As I previously stated, I was in foster care and later adopted. To some, this is one form of trauma and to others, it is not. Some children can have very loving and nurturing families. Others continue to long for what was lost. I can remember very few experiences of being in foster care. There was one incident where I was standing on a porch crying when my brother had to leave after our visit. My brother and I lived in separate foster homes. I can still visualize him pulling off in the car with his social worker.

The next memory I can recall was of me being in preschool. When I arrived home from school, I ate my peanut butter and jelly sandwich then went to take a nap. I can remember bumping my head on my pillow during my nap. My grandmother would come to the end of the stairs and yell at me to stop and go to sleep. I know now that bumping my head was a way to self-soothe.

What are things you have done to self-soothe?

_____

_____

_____

Growing up, I lived with my grandmother, two uncles, brother, and sister. The only thing that kept me in the realization that I was still a part of the foster care system was my foster care worker Ms. Ellis. She would visit us, I suppose monthly. For some reason, I never remember her being inside the house. I wonder what would have happened if she knew exactly what was going on in the walls of the home.

I would see her sitting in her car across the street from my house as I would walk home from school. It was because of Ms. Ellis that I wanted to be a foster care worker. That dream did come to pass many years later. I was a foster care worker for the state of Michigan, and I hated it. For me, it was just a system, one that was not leaving a positive impact on the youth it served.

Did you ever have a dream job and once you started working in the field, you hated it? Or did you love it like you thought you would?

I lived in a house that I believed to be in a nice neighborhood. Three bedrooms, an upstairs where I slept, a basement where I played with my dolls and a den where I watched my favorite shows, such as *The Cosby Show*. All my friends had a two-parent home. My grandmother did not work and was a single parent. I figured I had to be lucky to live on the block with the other families. I was raised in church. I played outside, made mud pies, rode my bike, jumped gates and from garages. I was a typical girl.

When I was growing up, black ants were enormous. They were not tiny like we see today. I can remember one of my neighbors put an ant in my sister's mouth. I was heated. I waited for my grandmother to leave the house, and I asked my neighbor to get the girl who did it. I tried to talk to her first, but at some point, I began to swing on her. It was no way you were going to mistreat my sister. It is funny because the moment she scratched me, I stopped the fight and went inside of the house to look in the mirror. I wanted to make sure I did not have a scratch on my face.

I wish I could say that was my last fight. Unfortunately, it was not. I can remember fighting another neighbor because he was not playing a game the way I wanted him to play it. Sorry Chucky! I may have had a few other fights in elementary school as well. I didn't know at the time that wanting control was a trauma response. To my future husband reading this, God is working on me with my control issues, please do not be afraid.

When you experience trauma, you feel powerless, voiceless, and hopeless. When you have the opportunity, you fight to regain it. Then someone enters your life and shows you that you are safe, that your voice matters and that you know longer have to fight. This person can be a friend, therapist, mate, or anyone in your life who cares for you or simply the word of God can bring you comfort and security.

I briefly mentioned being in foster care and later adopted. *Have any of you reading this been in foster care?*

How has it changed or impacted your life?

_____

_____

_____

_____

_____

Working with the youth I served in foster care broke my heart. They always had hopes that their parents would come back for them. I ran into several of those youth after they had aged out. Some ended up with family, but it was an aunt or an uncle, never their bio parents. Despite the trauma I have endured, I will say that I am happy that I was adopted. My parents were teenagers when I was born. I am not sure how my life would have turned out if they raised me. I assume they did the best they could, but would it have been what was best for me?

Growing up in an adopted home, there were some things about my life I knew and other things I did not. I knew my mother's name but not what she looked like. I did not know why we were taken from her. I knew I had a father who drove a cab and came around sometimes. If I can remember correctly, it was not a pleasant experience when he came around. There were times when he was drunk and causing arguments. He was the father of my sister and me, while my brother had his own father. Or so this is what I was told. We lived with my father's mother and two of his siblings. She did not want us separated so she adopted the three of us. For that, I am thankful.

However, within the walls of our home, we faced some challenges. A child should feel safe inside the walls of their home. They should feel loved and protected. Unfortunately, there are so many children who are abused, violated and unloved. I would like to think that parents do the best that they can. That may or may not be the truth. As a parent, I had to teach myself to be better, different for the next generation.

Growing up, my home was filled with pictures on the dining room walls and over the fireplace. These pictures,

along with Christmas and my Cabbage Patch dolls, were some of my favorite parts of childhood. Staying up late on Christmas Eve, waking up early and running down the stairs with excitement of opening our gifts. Goodfellow boxes, new bikes and of course, Cabbage Patch dolls were underneath the Christmas tree. Who could ask for a better childhood, right? I carried a big smile, but there were some challenges within the home that caused so much pain behind the smile.

As a child, I did not believe I was loved. I was told that I was just an average girl. I couldn't get good grades. I was never acknowledged for my birthday, and I was called names such as stupid. I wondered what my grandmother's life was like growing up. How was she treated?

I reached a point in my life where I was overwhelmed with emotions and taking the pills was my last resort. Years prior I began to cut my wrist. Nobody ever noticed, my grandmother, my teachers or my pastor, nobody. I was crying out for help, but I was not crying loud enough. I locked my feelings away into my many journals. Those journals housed so much pain that I eventually took them all and burned them in the backyard.

The person who had molested me had reentered my life. My grandmother must have known that he was doing it, right? This was something I considered, and I prayed it was not true. Because if she knew, why didn't she protect me? I took the bottle, yes, the entire bottle of pills because I was crying out to be seen. I always felt so invisible.

Have you ever felt invisible in your home? What did you do to be seen by others?

_____

_____

_____

_____

Sadly, like so many other boys and girls, a family member molested me. It grieves me to this day to think about the number of children who have been and are being sexually abused.

I am reminded of a time that he had me in his bed. An adult came up to his room and asked him to clean it. He had thrown the cover over my head so I would not be seen. Who cannot see a full body under the covers? It was at that moment I knew that there was no help for me.

My molester left the home for some time. While he was gone, I suppressed the memories. Sometime after his return, I began to remember the abuse. The first time I remembered through a dream. It was so vivid and so clear. I wrote my grandmother a letter to tell her. To my knowledge, she did not read it. I went to my pastor at the time; he told me that it was just a dream, and it was not real. Who was going to help me manage all these big emotions I was feeling? Who was going to protect me? Who was going to cry for the little girl?

I just had to cry for myself. Even after directly telling my grandmother what happened to me, she acted as if it didn't happen. I can understand it being hard to hear that the child you were supposed to protect was sexually abused. I do not know what I wanted or needed from her, other than to be heard. I just needed to be heard.

Have you experienced a situation in your life, and you did not feel like you were heard? How did you handle it?

_____

_____

_____

_____

_____

_____

While I was already working through the impact of my sexual abuse, another blow struck me. My sister and I were outside, and I saw a little boy running to our front door. He hopped out of the conversion van, knocked on my door and asked my sister and I for my older brother by name.

"He doesn't live here," I said.

He ran across the street to the next house.

"Wait a minute," I said, "What do you want with my brother?"

"I'm his brother," he said.

A woman opened the door to the van.

"I knew it was you; I knew it. I know that face," she shouted.

The woman in that van was my maternal grandmother.

At this time, I was sixteen and I was meeting a family that I did not know existed. I wish I could say that my life was full of roses and butterflies after that. But it was not. It was a whirlwind of emotions.

The days following that event were full of unknown adventures. That day my grandmother explained that when I was adopted, she remembered the area I lived in, but not the house. Which is why my brother was going door to door. He knew he had siblings and wanted to meet them. I later found out that my mother had six kids in total. Two girls and four boys.

My maternal grandmother gave me my mother's phone number. At this age, I had no idea how my mother looked or the sound of her voice. For years I would check the obituary section of the newspaper to see if she were alive.

I finally had my answer, she was alive and well, living on the east side of Detroit.

At the time I worked at McDonald's across from Northland Mall. I was at the register ringing up customers and I see a man just smiling at me. This was the moment my heart was shattered. Just looking at the man, I knew he was my birth father. I looked just like him. There was no question. The problem with this is that he was not the man that I had known as my father all these years. He was not my grandmother's son. He was a stranger who had my face.

I never had visions of meeting my father because I did not know he was someone I needed to meet. I thought I already knew him. I wanted to know who my dad was and why did I think someone else was? Shortly after that encounter, I met the woman I had been thinking about all my life, my mother. This reunion between my mother and I took place at the same location as my dad, in the lobby of McDonald's.

This began my identity crisis.

"Who was I?"

"So, my father isn't my father?"

"My family isn't my blood family?"

"Is that why my uncle molested me, because I wasn't really his niece, and he knew it."

"Were they ever going to tell me?"

I continued conversation with my little brother. It was because of him that we were all reunited. He had siblings and wanted to meet us. He was so mature to be so young. You know how you pray for something and think God does not hear you. For years I prayed to meet my mother, and I was now living in that answered prayer. Read Jeremiah 29:12.

You think I would be happy after finally meeting my maternal grandmother, brother, and my parents. But I was trapped in my emotions,

"Why did my mother keep her other kids and not us?"

"Why did they get to know her, and I didn't?"

I had so many questions and no answers.

I reached a point where I could no longer live in my childhood home. I was constantly reminded of my abuse. So late one evening, I left my grandmother's home. I packed one bag and grabbed my jar of seashells. My intention was to go to my male best friend's house. I could not find his house because it was dark outside, I couldn't see it. I had only walked to his house during the day. I was in the Grand River and Greenfield area on the streets all alone. Men kept stopping, thinking I was a prostitute. If I did not know prostitution was real, I knew that night.

I called my older brother so that he could come and pick me up. Since meeting our mom, he had moved in with her. He and my stepdad came to pick me up. When I woke up that morning, I was in a whole new world. Living there did not bring me anymore joy or peace. It only added to my pain.

I witnessed domestic violence, drugs, illegal transactions and much more. I had been so sheltered as a child that I had no clue what world I had entered. The last straw was when my older brother put his hands on me. The one thing I was not going to let a man do is beat me. I found myself once again packing my bags and leaving yet another home. As I think about it, this was my third time running away. The very first time, I left my grandmother's home and tried to escape to my aunt's house. This is when I first began to remember my sexual abuse. The police officers came and made me go back home.

These incidents of leaving home make me think about the videos I recently watched on social media. Women on the streets of Detroit who are prostitutes. Some have run away from home and never returned. Many admitted being sexually abused by family members. Some believe that the streets are better than the homes they came from. As I think about this, I just thank God for what he saved me from. I was one step away from the streets.

When I left my mother's house early that morning, I was at risk of becoming homeless and I was only seventeen. I had no plan; my only plan was just not to return to my mother or my grandmother's home. I stayed a few nights with my boyfriend when a childhood friend caught word of where I was living, she said not so. She invited me to move in with her. She lived with a high school friend and her mom. Her mom agreed to let me move in. I now live in a home with three strangers. Although I had known my friend for years, you really do not know a person until you live with them.

This woman, Ms. Allen, who I did not know, opened her doors to me. If I had never experienced Gods love through a stranger before, I did during that season. She opened her home, her heart, and her family to me. Her daughter, Jennifer, is now one of my best friends. With all the love they had given me in that home, I was still hurting and still lost. My trauma hunted me daily.

Growing up, experiencing multiple forms of trauma was just my life. Foster care, adoption, being bullied, sexual molestation, never being told I love you or even feeling loved. Being told that I was stupid, never being acknowledged for my birthday, never feeling like I mattered, being beat. This was my life.

By the time I was 18 I had a baby, a boyfriend (a few years later he became my husband) and on my way to living on my own. I could hide my scars and my pain, but only for so long. After five years of my relationship. My trauma

finally came to the light. I do not know if my husband saw it, but I did and heard it loud and clear. I had been hiding from myself for so long that I could no longer do it.

After my divorce, I lost my mind. I began to drink to the point where I ended up in the hospital, caring about absolutely nothing and no one. I was lost, trying to heal and find my identity at the same time. Scripture says that our bodies are not our own. They belong to God. They are the temple of the holy spirit. Read 1 Corinthians 6:19-20

I know that now, but at the time, I thought my body was my own. I abused it. I mistreated it and I let men misuse and abuse it.

I had a season where I slept with whoever I wanted to when I wanted to. I suppose I wanted control over my body and my life. When you are molested and sexual assaulted, your power is taken away from you. When you get the opportunity, you fight so hard to regain that power and control. I thought I had control, but the only control I had was over destroying my temple. I was so lost and spiraling out of control. I knew that I was in a bad place when one neighbor asked another neighbor if he was my pimp. That neighbor hung out on my porch a lot. When I met him, he was selling weed out of his station wagon. I was so naïve that I did not realize that he was using my house as, "the spot" and he was actually the weed man.

One of my neighbors noticed that the weed man was on my porch a lot and he observed different men hanging out. He automatically assumed that I was a prostitute, and the weed man was my pimp. What he didn't realize is that a lot of men were there for the weed man, but it did not look good to someone outside looking in. However, I was so ashamed of my life. I know longer recognized myself and I was so far from God. No matter how far I was from God, he never stopped being close to me.

That year was an absolute nightmare. Being in the hospital, getting drunk, being taken advantage of, and clubbing all the time. What was I doing with my life? One night after leaving the club, two young men came to my house. I have no idea why they were there because none of my friends were with me. I am sure you can imagine what could have happened to me. I remember being so drunk that I rolled off my porch, down the cement stairs and all the way to the curb.

The young men called 911, then burned rubber behind me. The EMS came and laid me in my front room. They put the little ammonia pack under my nose to help me wake up. "Oh, she's just drunk, there's nothing wrong with her, she just wants attention.'' They gathered their things and left me on the floor of my home. Something was wrong with me, but they could not help me. Here I was in my twenties, ignoring the abuse that I experienced as a child. Instead of admitting it happened and allowing God to heal me, I had the spirit of amnesia. I wanted to forget it all. I tried to let sex and alcohol heal me.

My story is not over, sex and alcohol did not win. I eventually began to calm down some. A young man came into my life and would go on to be my second husband. This was something I would feel ashamed of, being so young and already married twice. Robert's entry into my life ended my cycle of losing my mind. His presence saved me from the cycle I was in, but he did not save me from my sin.

We had only been dating a few months before our child began to grow in my womb. My boyfriend and I walked into the clinic, and they sent us to the examination room. They showed us the ultrasound of our child that had already begun to develop. Lying on the table to end our child's life, I realized how far away from God I was. I always disagreed with abortion, but here I was, ending the life of a child that God knew before they were in my womb. It grieved me, but I continued to live my life of sin. Robert eventually broke things off with me because he decided to live his life for God. I wanted to live for God again too, but I was still tangled up in the world.

One night a friend and I headed downtown to a club. We parked at a hotel down the road then walked to the club. We had on our usual tight jeans, low cut shirts showing off our tattoos and I opted for a pair of flats instead of heals. We walked into the club ready to have a good time (although I secretly never had a good time). As I walked to the club a piece of glass went through my shoe and stabbed the bottom of my foot.

I cleaned up my foot then began to rock to the beat of the song,

" *Said I'm outside of the club and you think I'm a punk,*"

" *I ain't never scared, I ain't never scared*" we shouted and threw our hands up to the song. This was my song!

Shortly after, we began hearing gunshots. We all rushed out of the club. As we walked to my car, we noticed that it was not there. It was towed because I wasn't authorized to park in the hotel lot where we parked. I knew I never wanted to go to a club again. But what I did not know is that weeks later, I would give my life to God.

I went to see my ex-boyfriend's mother for her birthday. I wanted to drop her off a gospel CD. During my visit, she invited me to church for Monday night prayer, which was the next day, October 20, 2003. I went to prayer and my life changed. That evening at Soul Deliverance church, I spoke in tongues for the first time and was baptized in Jesus' name. My life changed instantly. Some of my friends would say, 'It's no way you have changed." But what I felt in the moments of my baptism was love. "For God so loved the world that he gave his only son and whosoever believed on him should not perish but have everlasting life" (John 3:16).

His love took me captive and saved my soul. Even when I did not love myself. My sin did not end his love for me. He did not stop loving me and he never stopped calling me. Scripture says, 'Before I formed you in your mother's womb I knew you, before you were born, I set you apart." I appointed you..." (Jeremiah 1:5).

God knew us before we were ever in our mothers womb, he called us and set us apart. If you are reading this and you or someone you know has experienced trauma, I am so sorry. Please know that your trauma does not define you. It is not the end of your story. With the help of God and therapy you can change your story from trauma to triumph. God loves you and he is waiting to heal your broken pieces.

After reading my story, please know that I have no unforgiveness or hate in my heart for anyone. God is allowing me to turn my story into a testimony and help you all know that healing belongs to you. The trauma that I have experienced does not make me bitter. It has only fueled me to help the next generation. Trauma did not win in my life and it doesn't have to win in yours. Pray with me.

Dear God,

Bless my sister/brother whose hands touched this book. Bless every word that it may penetrate their heart and lead them to a place of healing, acceptance, love, and peace. Bless the chains and shackles that have been holding them hostage, that they may break. The generational curse ends with them, the generational trauma ends with them, the healing starts with them. Their home will be blessed, their family will be blessed! Wrap them in your arms and turn their heart of stone into flesh. Lord, we thank you in advance for your healing.

In Jesus Name, Amen

Trauma to Triumph

Author Karla Young

"You are so stupid."

"I can't believe you're so dumb.''

At an early age, being called dumb, stupid, and being belittled was just the beginning of my trauma. The sting of the extension cord against my bare skin left a trail of scars, a road map of pain edged into my flesh, but this is not my identity.

I am Karla. I experienced trauma in my childhood, as early as 3 years old. This is not just a story of trauma. It is a testament to the resilience of the human spirit and overcoming my trauma. I was once broken but not destroyed.

Sharing my personal story of overcoming trauma is essential for several reasons. I believe sharing my experience can help break the shame surrounding it and can serve as a source of inspiration and hope for others who may be going through similar experiences. It demonstrates that healing from trauma is possible and that there is a light at the end of the tunnel. It is also a way to connect with others, raise awareness, and contribute to a more supportive and understanding community.

My Story

I was born into a two-parent household in Detroit, Michigan, the third youngest of four. What set my story apart from so many is that I was born naturally but had unseen disabilities that were later found in life. I was born with a speech impediment, a condition that impacts an individual's ability to speak fluently, correctly, or with a clear resonance or tone.

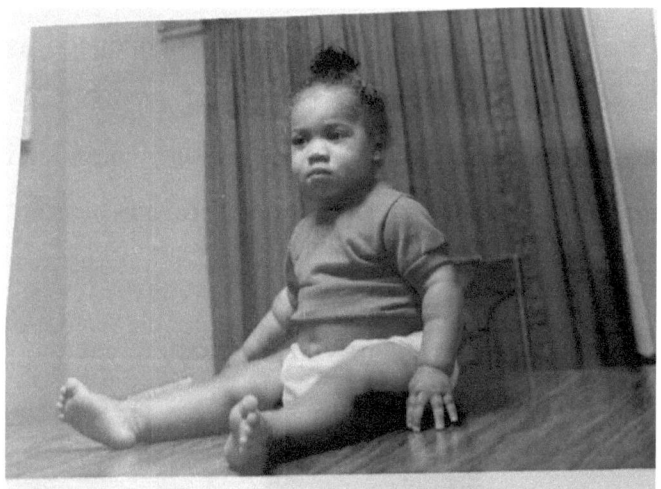

My disabilities were the beginning of my trauma and the cause of most of my whippings.

Dealing with Trauma Drama:

A gripping, scary, dangerous, violent, emotional, and unexpected series of events.

I remember a time when my mother was preparing me for kindergarten. I was sitting at our rustic brown kitchen table with my knees on the chair too short to comfortably reach over the table to write my name, address, and phone number. I remember the tremble in my tiny fingers, fearful of making any mistakes that might earn me a whipping. My mother kept my father's sturdy black belt on the table, ready to use for my next whipping. I could not achieve what my mother was hoping for. I just could not do it. Every time I made a mistake, I would receive a stinging whip across my legs. I was whipped until my body went numb, trembling uncontrollably. My face was swollen and smeared with snot from all the crying. Imagine being told not to cry; that is what I was told, "and you better not cry!" I had to weep silently, often cupping my mouth with my tiny hands to stifle the sound. I was petrified and in shock from seeing the bloody welts on my legs, looking like train tracks where the black belt had torn into my flesh. It was always a trigger for me to see the color black, let alone a belt.

What are some things from your past that cause you to be triggered? How do you handle your triggers?

_____

_____

_____

_____

_____

_____

"She did it."

My siblings took advantage of my struggles of not being able to talk and defend myself. I became their scapegoat and would be blamed for things they did. Once, my sisters accidentally spilled sugar all over our kitchen floor while I was upstairs playing, utterly unaware of the situation. When my mom asked what had happened and who did it, my sisters blamed me. With my gibberish talk, unable to get an understandable word out. I was choked, slapped, and beaten up on our blue-carpeted stairs that led to my bedroom where I stayed.

I was treated as if I did not belong, the black sheep of my family. My siblings would tease me and say that I was purchased off the shelf of a grocery store by my parents, and

I believed it because of the beatings I endured. I believed the lie.

One of the strongest survival mechanisms I remember was watching a movie called, *Roots*. I wanted to see how they had survived their beatings. I picked up a saying that caused the individual to stop being whipped. "I kiss your feet." Those were the very first words I could get out of my mouth. That became my plea to my mom each time she whipped me. I would fall to my knees, grab hold of one of her legs, latch on, and hug it as she dragged me to where the belt was, screaming,

"I kiss your feet."

"I kiss your feet."

"I kiss your feet."

repeatedly hoping she would have mercy on me.

The home that once made me feel safe became a source of my torment. I despised being there. The walls enclosed the house and the burden of my suffering. The only thing I had trust in was the dolls that I played with and confided in.

I have always had a love for being outside the walls of my house. It was the safest space for me, and I found peace outside my home. The open sky and the wind were my companions, offering me a sense of peace and freedom. They provided refuge from my life within those walls, until the moment came when I was asked to pick a switch from the tree to be whipped with. Just to break the inner thigh of my skin.

I did not feel safe with anyone. I had no trust in any person. I only trusted the dolls I played with and confided in. I knew my secret of being abused would not get out, that was my greatest fear.

My parents faced numerous struggles, unable to provide the nurturing environment I desperately needed. Eventually they divorced, and we moved to my mother's hometown. I had a glimpse of hope, believing the beatings might cease in this new setting. Unfortunately, they continued. The trauma I experienced affected me in several areas and stages of my life.

My school years

Once I started school, it was a challenging experience for me, marked by trauma that pushed me to strive for perfection in everything I did. I was a nervous wreck and had no confidence in anything I did. I became an overachiever, constantly aiming to please others despite struggling with low self-esteem and trust issues that shadowed my every move. I became very shy and withdrawn. Concentrating in class was impossible. The looming threat of a whooping at home consumed my thoughts. My shyness and lack of confidence only grew. I found myself easily startled by the most minor things.

My focus and concentration on schoolwork were distorted and destroyed so much that I failed fifth grade. The more beatings I would receive at home, the more I carried that pain and anger to school. By the time I started middle school, these challenges manifested as aggressive behavior, often leading to conflicts and fights to the point where I was kicked out of school on many occasions. I was eventually put into adolescent counseling. I hid behind the dark pain that lay just beneath my skin of the bruises, too afraid and ashamed to tell any of my trauma drama.

One thing that I learned while receiving counseling (still holding onto my secret of abuse) was to start journaling. It was the most powerful tool that helped me through my experience. Journaling was therapeutic and gave me a safe space to express my emotions and get them off my chest instead of holding things in and exploding onto others. Journaling helped me throughout the rest of middle school.

Despite everything, I was very likable in school. Teachers and classmates saw potential in me but misunderstood the turmoil within. Behind the facade of the likable student was a child hiding behind layers of pain, too scared to reveal the true extent of my suffering.

In high school, I started looking for love in the wrong places and seeking validation and approval from others. This led me to make poor decisions in my early teens and I became pregnant at age 16. Hiding my pregnancy for several months in fear of what my mother would do to me. In my head, I thought it was a way to get back at my mom and show her how to love and treat a child.

As a Parent

Fast forward to me becoming a parent, the trauma and mistreatment from my mother finally ceased. Though she began to treat me as an adult, she remained strict and controlling. At that time, I was in the 11th grade, technically free from my mother's custody but not yet old enough to legally live on my own. Consequently, I continued to reside under her roof until I reached the appropriate age to move out.

In 1993, I finally moved out, embracing my newfound independence. Surprisingly, my relationship with my mother improved significantly. Despite this, I lived unaware and unhealed, believing I could simply erase the painful memories by not thinking or talking about them. However, trauma does not vanish so quickly. It lay dormant, hidden beneath the surface of unseen wounds.

I discovered the hard way, that you cannot simply sweep trauma under the rug and hope that it will just go away or be forgotten.

As an adult parent, I continued to live life recklessly. I found myself repeating the same destructive behaviors I had exhibited while living with my mother. Alarmingly, I

started to notice these patterns emerging in my interactions with my children.

Such as slapping my children. I realized I was treating my children the way my mother treated me. Recognizing this, I quickly sought out parenting classes, determined to break the cycle and provide a healthier environment for my kids.

Work-life

Growing up with unresolved childhood trauma profoundly shaped the way I operated in the workplace. Wounds often guided my behavior, emotions, and relationships with co-workers I had not yet confronted. One of the clear signs of this was how sensitive I became to criticism. What others saw as simple feedback, I perceived it as personal attacks. This defensiveness would often lead me to emotional outbursts and a sense of stress.

There is one moment I will never forget when my supervisor gave me instructions on handling a task. She was there to help me. Instead of taking it in stride, I felt anger building inside me. I became so emotionally charged that I lashed out, telling her, "You're running through my bloodstream, you're getting on my last nerves, and I'm ready to fight." I was not fully aware of my emotional state, but something about my words must have alarmed her. Instead of disciplining me, I was sent home, realizing I was going through something much more profound. Something I did not fully understand myself.

Trust was a huge challenge for me. I found it difficult to trust colleagues, supervisors, or anyone with authority. It brought me back to remembering my history with my mother being an authoritative figure in my life. It was as if my past trauma filtered every interaction, making me feel unsafe and misunderstood. Simple teamwork or following directions became battles. I rarely asked for help, and instead, I worked as if I knew it all. I knew nothing. I had no room for growth, and in fact, in truth, I was much more afraid of seeming weak or incapable of being reminded that I was so stupid and couldn't believe how dumb I was.

Over time, this unresolved pain began to manifest in more ways. I developed anxiety and depression, which affected my performance. My boss received more complaints about me daily. I would call off work more frequently, struggle to concentrate, and often feel overwhelmed. Small things would trigger me, dragging me back to past traumas. This constant state of emotional tension has affected my professionalism. I threw myself into work to prove my worth as both a perfectionist and a workaholic. Though this seemed like dedication, it led me to burn out and immediately walk out and quit jobs.

My trauma made it hard to see people's intentions. I often misinterpreted others' words or actions as threats, leading to unnecessary conflict and strained communication. I struggled with seeing that not every challenge or confrontation was rooted in harm.

Yet, through it all, I see God's hand at work. He allowed me to go through these challenges, not to break but to heal me. Through self-reflection, prayer, and learning to trust him, I began to understand that my trauma did not define me. In the workplace, I realized that my true value and strength did not come from perfection or hard work alone but from leaning on God and trusting him to guide my steps.

Fast forward, with all the flashbacks of my past childhood trauma and memories, I decided to forgive my mother (so I thought) until it returned. The day I questioned my life, I felt I had been born by mistake. I did not feel a sense of belonging, which led me to revisit my spiritual life. I went seeking it a year before Covid hit, leading me down a dark path and into a pit that broke me, still not knowing what was breaking me until I stumbled upon the old journals of my childhood life. I didn't like what I was reading, and as I stood in my backyard staring at the flames of the fire pit, I ran into the house to grab my past hurt journals and burn the memory right out of my life, not knowing the pain still lay beneath the unseen scars etched into my flesh.

I was desperately trying to heal a wound that seemed impossible to mend on my own. I reached out to the world's remedies, grasping at anything that promised relief. Clutching crystals, practicing self-healing through Reiki, and delving into inner child work. Healing the world's way had no power or substance. Each step and attempt felt like a lifeline, but I spiraled further into darkness instead of finding solace. The pain grew heavier, more suffocating, until it became too much to bear. The weight of it all finally broke me, and I shattered, spiraling into a nervous breakdown.

My healing journey ignited when I heard the Holy Spirit's voice clear, which was powerful and life changing. "You cannot heal without the Healer," he said, and in that instant, a spark of hope ignited within me. I was trying to be perfect without the perfect one and trying to heal the inner child without the healer, Jesus Christ. It was as if the air around me shifted, filled with possibility and light.

Psalm 147:3 came alive in my heart: "He heals the brokenhearted and binds up their wounds." I felt those words wrapping around my heart like a warm embrace, mending the broken pieces and infusing me with new strength.

Then came the promise of Psalm 34:18, a beacon that pierced through the darkness: "The Lord is close to the brokenhearted and saves those who are crushed in spirit." The realization hit me like a wave of pure relief, the Lord was not just near; he was right beside me, lifting me when I thought I could not go on. It was like breathing in life, filling my spirit with energy and purpose.

With this divine guidance, I was led to seek out the best of the best in therapy, who would help me navigate the most difficult chapters of my life. And through every challenging moment, I knew I was not alone. The Lord was my constant companion, cheering me on, holding me up, and leading me down the true path to healing. What once felt impossible now seemed not only achievable but inevitable. I was on the road to complete restoration, and nothing could stop me.

One thing that the Holy Spirit showed me was taking accountability for myself.

HEALING IS WORTH MY FREEDOM

Looking back on my life, as difficult as some moments may have been, I can now acknowledge with an open heart that my mother did her best. It was not always easy, but I have come to understand her actions in a way that allows me to embrace both the pain and the healing that followed.

As we have had many conversations since I left home, my mother has shared stories of her childhood trauma. I have seen how the experiences she endured shaped her parenting, and while there were painful moments, I now realize that her actions were not born from malice but from a desire to protect me from the same suffering she had gone through. She was not making excuses, nor am I. My mother wanted better for me even if her methods, at times, were misguided. She believed she was preparing me for Life, trying to equip me to face the challenges she knew all too well. Yet, in retrospect, she recognizes that her path was flawed. She has expressed deep remorse for the pain she caused, and I know her apology comes from a place of genuine regret.

In my maturity, I have learned to pull some treasures from the pain and see the positive hidden within the difficult moments. I have become someone who is organized, resilient, and determined. My mother helped shape these qualities in me, and for that, I am grateful. I have learned to be a leader, to never give up on the things I care about, and most importantly, I have learned that I am an overcomer who can achieve anything I set my mind to.

I now see my mother parented me from a place of pain. Pain was not hers alone to bear but was passed down from generation to generation. The struggles she faced affected how she raised me, but I can see now that it was not because my mother did not love me; it was because my mother was still carrying unhealed wounds of her own. She did not have the tools to heal before becoming a parent, and I can only imagine how overwhelming that must have been for her.

It may sound like I am defending her, but I offer understanding. My mother genuinely believed she was doing the right thing. Though it hurt at times, I cannot ignore the love and intention behind her actions. She has since apologized, time and time again, for the pain she caused, and I know those apologies come from a place of deep sincerity. We can't change the past, but I believe in the possibility of a better future. One filled with understanding, love, and support.

Today, my mother and I share a stronger bond than ever. She is my best friend, my confident confidante, and someone I hold close to my heart. I bear no grudges, no bitterness, no anger. I see her now not just as my mother but as a woman who has endured so much and has grown in her healing journey. Despite it all, I love her dearly because I have become the best version of myself.

The good in my life far outweighs the bad. I have nothing but compassion for my mother. I have seen her pain, and she has seen mine. Together, we move forward with empathy, healing the wounds we both carried. With that understanding, we honor the struggles of the past without letting them define our future. My heart is full of love and peace; my mother will always be the center of that.

I encourage and challenge others to heal from childhood trauma; it is a delicate and compassionate process. Be patient with yourself.

Tips for healing

1. Acknowledge the pain and its impact; allowing yourself to feel the emotions that come with your past is essential. Do not minimize what you went through. It is valid, and it matters. You cannot heal what you do not admit.

2. Understand that healing is a process; healing is not linear, and taking things slow is okay. Be kind to yourself during this process and remember that every small step forward is progress. Be without judgment or pressure.

3. Seek professional help if you feel ready; talking to a therapist or counselor can be incredibly helpful. They can provide you with the tools to navigate your trauma and help you find your way to Healing. In our culture, African Americans shunned therapists, and it is seen as a shameful thing, but there is nothing to be ashamed of; they are there to help, and a therapist can provide guidance, coping mechanisms, and a safe space to process painful memories.

4. Break the cycle of generational trauma. Know that you have the power to break the cycle of trauma. By focusing on your healing, you are helping yourself and creating a healthier future for those around you.

5. Practice self-compassion- Be gentle with yourself. Healing from trauma can stir up feelings of shame or guilt but remember that you are worthy of love and care, especially from yourself.

6. Surround yourself with supportive people; find people who make you feel safe, heard, and valued. It is okay to distance yourself from those who trigger your trauma or make you feel unsafe.

7. Reconnect with your heart; reconnecting with your heart through gentle practice like mindfulness and meditation on the word of God can help you feel grounded and more in control of Your healing. Spend time in silence, away from distractions, and listen to your heart.

8. Journaling and reflecting: Journaling is a great way to express what's inside; sometimes, writing things down brings clarity and relief. Even if it is just for you, it is a significant weight lifted from your shoulders once it is released safely and positively.

9. Embrace small victories; celebrate the little wins, whether setting boundaries, expressing your feelings, or simply getting through a tough day. Every step forward matters.

10. Healing is worth it; healing can be challenging, but it is worth the freedom and peace you will have. On the other hand, it will allow you to live a life that is not defined by your trauma.

Forgiveness is a crucial step in healing trauma; it marks the true beginning of the healing process. Start by forgiving yourself for allowing the trauma to take control over your life. Then, gradually extend forgiveness to everyone who has caused you pain or harm. With healing come lessons, blessings, and wisdom. In doing so, you free yourself from the grip of the past and open the door to more profound healing. Ephesians 4:31-32 says, "Let all bitterness, and wrath, and anger, clamor [perpetual hate, resentment, strife, fault-finding], and slander be put away from you, along with every kind of malice [all spitefulness, verbal abuse, malevolence]. Be kind and helpful to one another, tender-hearted [compassionate, understanding], forgiving one another [readily and freely], just as God in Christ also forgave you.

Purpose statement

The purpose of my book is to share my personal journey of healing from childhood trauma, giving God all the glory for the restoration he has brought into my life. Through my testimony, I encourage both those who already believe in Christ Jesus and those who are searching for Hope and healing, regardless of their faith background.

For believers, I want to reaffirm the power of God's love, grace, and redemption, showing how he can bring us through even the darkest valleys when we surrender to him.

For unbelievers, I aim to offer an open and honest account of my experience, allowing them to see how faith in Christ transformed my life, with the hope that they too, might find healing and restoration in their own lives.

By sharing my story, I pray that it will serve as a source of comfort, strength, and inspiration for anyone who has experienced childhood trauma or any trauma of a kind. My desire is to show that healing is possible, and through God, we can overcome the pain of the past and walk into a future filled with hope. My prayer for you is...

A Prayer for Healing from Childhood Trauma

Dear God,

I come to you today with a heavy heart, lifting the person who has endured the pain and burden of past childhood trauma. Lord, you know the depths of their suffering and the scars that linger both seen and unseen. I ask that you surround them with your love and comfort in this healing time.

Grant them the strength to face the wounds of their past and give them the courage to confront their pain without fear. Lord, let them feel your presence in the darkest moments, reminding them That they are never alone. Lord, that you will never leave them nor forsake them. Feel their heart with the peace that surpasses all understanding and gently guides them toward wholeness. You are a God that heals.

I pray for patience as they embark on this healing journey, knowing it will take time. Help them to be kind to themselves, embrace the process, and trust in your plan for their life. May they learn to forgive those who have caused harm, and may they also learn to forgive themselves for any pain they may carry. Lord, please bring people into their lives who will support them with compassion, understanding, and love. Surround them with positive influences that uplift their spirit and encourage growth. May they find strength in community, wisdom in their experiences, and hope for a brighter future. Above all, remind them of their worth. Remind them that they are loved that they are valued, and that they are deserving of healing and joy. Help them to see themselves through your eyes as precious and whole, even in their brokenness. We Trust in your healing power, Lord, and we believe you can restore the parts of yourself that have been hurt. Please continue to walk with them on this path to freedom from the past, and may your love be their guiding light. In your holy name, I pray, amen.

This prayer asks for strength, peace, patience, love, and trust in God's healing and restoration power.

May God peace and healing be with you. I can be reached at karlab4real@yahoo.com

Religious Trauma

Author Melonie Hobbs

RELIGIOUS TRAUMA

"Giving honor to God, who is the head of my life. To my pastor, first lady, and all the saints and friends. I am glad to be in the service one mo' time. I could'a been dead, sleeping in my grave. But God made ole death behave. God, I thank you for being a bridge over troubled waters. A mother to the motherless and a father to the fatherless. A doctor in the sick room and a lawyer in the courtroom. He is everything to me. Pray for me as I grow stronger in the Lord."

A script I learned as a child to express my testimony of God, which led me on a path to discovery. I wanted so much to please God, know more about him, and serve those who had ruled over me. I started to watch and obey all things from leadership and those in high positions within the church community. Watching them from near and far led me down a path to imitate all things presented. I learned quickly, "Do as I say, not as I do." I followed to a fault and realized after doing some research and healing work, that I was a victim of religious trauma.

What is religious trauma? As a therapist practicing in Michigan, I started experiencing the root causes of certain symptoms I noticed in myself. I knew about church hurt and spiritual abuse, but I was unsure about religious trauma.

According to therapist.com, religious trauma is when a person's religious experience is stressful, degrading, dangerous, abusive, and damaging. Traumatic religious experiences may harm or threaten someone's physical, emotional, mental, sexual, or spiritual health and safety. Listed in the article there were ten symptoms of religious trauma: self-hatred, shame, perfectionism, hypervigilance, difficulty making decisions, loss of community, lack of boundaries, delayed social milestones, sexual dysfunction, and mental health disorders. After reading I decided to take a religious trauma quiz, and I discovered I have severe religious trauma. Honey child , I couldn't believe it.

I had so many symptoms of religious trauma, being raised in the church, a daughter of a Bishop and Evangelist Missionary. From childhood to adulthood, I realized I have experienced PTSD, depression, anxiety and more dealing with religious trauma. I recall growing up in church being there literally every day for rehearsals, cleaning, serving, soul witnessing, completing administration work and more. All my life I was taught to face life situations and circumstances through a religious lens and at the age of 38 years old I decided to see it differently from the lens as a runaway. Not a runaway from God but from the Christian religious systems. At such time I started my healing journey from religious trauma, and I am so glad that I did. I pray while you are reading you will allow me to take you on a journey as I reveal my life experiences of pain and suffering dealing with a lifespan of religious trauma. I pray my story blesses your life in a way that will resonate, empower, and motivate you to fully trust God, seek to know him authentically, trust him and allow him to heal your wounds. I hope you can see beauty in my ashes that led me to victory on this side of my journey.

Perfection

Growing up in the church, I heard things such as, "Who does she think she is? Sit up straight, close your legs you have on a dress, speak when spoken to, keep silent, slow to speak, quick to hear, speak when you are spoken to. Oh, my goodness, look at those tight-fitting clothes she has on.

She has no pantyhose on, honey you cannot lead worship. Look at that split; your clothes are too snug. Wait, look at her hair and nails. She is too young to be wearing that mess."

"Is that Melonie Fizer pregnant? I knew it!" These are just a few things the religious community would say to me that caused me to dress modestly and totally cover up in my youth and adult age. I did not want to cause any trouble for my parents or myself. I wanted to assure that I lived up to the church's expectations of me to continue to be the perfect church girl trophy to be admired. However, these ruminating thoughts caused me to shut down, have low self-esteem, compare myself to others, participate in negative self-talk, strive for perfection, and break down crying and talk to my mother about my feelings. My mother would encourage me by giving me the word of God, praying, grabbing my hand, and singing We are Going to Make It by Myrna Summers and Timothy Wright.

One time I remember my mother was feeling down and I made a conscious decision to erase her pain by becoming the perfect daughter. What does that mean? I would try my best not to cause her pain and anguish like I saw the church folks do, my father, friends, work and sometimes family too. I would try to do no wrong in the sight of the religious community, mother, and family. However, I was losing an eternal struggle with life being perfect in front of others yet imperfect behind closed doors. Yet, it was artificial, and I was genuine. I had a smile and was upright, like everything was ok and trust me it was not.

In my early 20s I remember singing with my musical family Antun Foster and Chemistry. During this time, there was a big focus from the religious community on what I wore and how I carried myself in the music industry. There were some who said that I was fast, and I dressed too grown for my age! You be the judge checkout the photo of me wearing fitted clothing with body shaped just right. Yet, I became hypervigilant and paranoid about my wardrobe covering up my body by wearing loose fitting clothing, covering up in hot places, discoloration on my legs, constantly being worried about my attire, not showing up fully in the  rooms, worried about revealing too much skin, causing PTSD and triggers. Again, I would do this to ensure I would not be talked about and to display perfection in the eyes of the church community. Please know my clothes were not too tight! My mother district missionary evangelist Pamela Fizer-Cry did not play that. As I reflect on these experiences, my mother could only purchase clothing on her single mother's salary. She would buy me clothes from Dots, Winkelman, Marians, K-mart and Meijers. I would ask for long summer dresses and add a jacket or sweater to assure coverage.

The lesson I learned in perfection: do not allow others' opinions to cause you to not show up fully in any room that you are in. Yes, dress appropriately for the king and not for people. The bible states, Galatians 1:10 "For do I now persuade men, or God? Or do I seek to please men? For if I yet pleased men, I should not be the servant of Christ" and Ephesians 6:6 "Not with eyeservice, as men pleasers; but as the servants of Christ, doing the will of God from the heart." Take words of wisdom then shred the rest. Allow God to direct every aspect of your life.

Shame

As I walked down the long hallway of my dorm room with my best friend, I began to get nervous. We stepped into the room, and I pulled out my bag and headed to the bathroom. I came out of the bathroom and my bestie went in after and slid down the door with intensified dramatics with a sad and surprised look on her face saying, "Mel you are pregnant!"

I was immediately shocked, and I could not respond from my continual laughter and denial. She immediately said Mel, you are the worship leader, pastor's reader, resident advisor, still in school. You must talk to the pastor etc. I knew I had to say something to my leader and instantly I started to feel anxiety and sadness.

So, I went to the clinic to get a second opinion and discovered on the ultrasound that my child had a heartbeat, hands, fingers, and toes looking like a fully developed baby. My drive back to the dorm was horrible. I screamed, cried, and told myself multiple times, "you're so stupid." I just knew that this would hurt my mother, father, family, religious community, and God by not following biblical precepts and examples. I felt like I embarrassed them and caused reproach to us all.

I made up in my mind I would talk to my leaders and stop being the worship leader. He then told me that I needed to apologize in front of the church. The doctor put me on bed rest for 4 months so when I returned to church I did as my pastor requested, however instead of apologizing. I thanked everyone who provided any aid and assistance to me during that time. People began to talk about me and hurt me with words causing me to feel shame and low self-esteem. I was even blackballed by the church community due to being pregnant outside of holy matrimony. The lessons I learned were so many ways to keep myself pure before God because of the love I have for him. People can be rude and cruel not understanding the mental turmoil an individual is going through, and that shame comes from knowing right from wrong and condemning oneself for not following biblical principles. Which reminds me of Adam and Eve after they had sinned, they went and hid due to guilt and shame.

Lesson, I learned to turn to God and apologized for my wrongdoings, asking him to save me and fill me again. That is all I needed to do and choose not to be entangled with the yoke of bondage again. People do not have a heaven or hell to put me in and only God can judge me. During that time, a song was birth through me called *Void*. In the song, I am crying to God to fill and heal the void in my heart. The bible scripture that encouraged me was Romans 8:1 "There is therefore now no condemnation for those who are in Christ Jesus."

Delayed Social Milestones

Can I keep it one hundred? I honestly started to turn up in my adult age. Shocking I know. Over time I developed delayed milestones causing me to delay in my ability to meet expected physical, cognitive, social, or emotional developmental stages. For example, I pulled up to a guest church for their cafe night and I found myself in a compromising situation. I initially went to sing, yet I was staring at a bottle of Hennessy. The peer pressure got real, "Mel do you want some of this? No thank you, I replied. I saw a boy I wanted to get close to and he waved at me from across the room, I thought to myself, sweet baby Jesus. I could not wait until after service.

When he came close to me, I would feel a tingling sensation and did not learn until my adult age that it was a horny symptom. All I knew was I just wanted to be close to him because it helped me to heal my father's womb of abandonment and loneliness.

This later caused me to yearn for more closeness with a man. Questioning sexuality and identity to heal me even if it was for a moment of satisfaction. Such behavior landed me in multiple broken relationships and in abusive relationship with a man that was bad, scaring me emotionally and mentally. This continued to cause me to experience a war internally to stay and go against what God wanted for me in relationships in and outside of the church. Religious trauma hindered my personal identity.

It discouraged me from exploring who I was outside of my faith. Everything I did was connected to my faith. This caused me delays in understanding personal values, beliefs, and a clear sense of self. The lesson I learned was to realize God despises sin, but he loves you. St. John 3:17 states "For God did not send his Son into the world to condemn the world, but in order that the world might be saved through him." I would just lean into the thoughts of hell and brimstone and judgement making me believe that God only had it out for me and not so. He is forgiving and loving, and he bears the infirmities of the weak.

Difficulty Making Decisions

I am sad to say due to my religious trauma and delays it caused me to be codependent. There were so many voices around me until I could not clearly define my own voice, making me feel like I was delayed while watching others in my group make decisions without approval. I allowed my mother, pastor, family, friends, and other church leaders to define my voice for me. I was an obedient daughter to all. I had to check in to do everything, from who I dated, where I worked or even who my friends were. I did not have much of a choice of my own. I constantly had to ask for approval which caused me to be codependent on others. I recall a time I wanted to switch jobs. I did not feel confident making the best decision for myself, so I called my leaders asking them to help me make the decision and they did. I felt bad I was unable to make that decision without the help of someone, which reminded me of a song by a famous gospel singer with lyrics, 'we fall down but we get up.' The lessons I learned: Get up no matter how far you have fallen. Rise and be healed and not delayed. Make your own decisions with God's help. You know what is best for you, so trust yourself. Value your thoughts and opinions with confidence and assurance.

Loss of Community

Born and raised in church from infancy to adulthood, all I knew was church! The church institution is a whole world within its community. Inside of the church community there are some spoken and unspoken rules, regulations, laws, policies and more. Thou shall not break any of them for if you do you just may lose your support and community. For example, when I got pregnant outside of holy matrimony, changed denomination, chose to follow my way opposite of the religious system, I lost my community. If you grow up singing or playing an instrument in church and go and lend your skills and talents to the world they will talk about you, rebuke you and possibly send you to hell. I transitioned from one denomination to another due to employment and the need for freedom. When the church folks got a hold of this information,

I lost a lot of my friends and family due to my choice. I was the girl in church every day of the week, assisting with making dinners, soul witnessing, cleaning the church, unlocking, and locking the doors, servant, leader and attending four services on Sundays. For example, Sunday School, morning worship, 4 o'clock service, night services/ Young People's Willing Workers.

The expectations were quite high. I gave it all to church and due to the people treating me that way they caused me to experience church hurt and because biblically people would use the word to further damage me. I decided to become a runaway. I became a runaway from the religious system, not God. I had to make it clear to my friends I love God, yet I wanted to see the church world outside of the lens of the church community. Lesson learned: choose people/community who choose you. Disconnect from toxic relationships and create boundaries and stick to them.

Self-Hatred

The religious community let me down and caused me many wounds. It caused me to judge, and second guess myself multiple times. I did not know I had these wounds until I decided to do my work on my quest to find healing from my religious trauma. The church's grand expectations caused me to feel and believe that it was achievable, causing me to hate myself for not being able to make my own choices, criticize myself for not having, living up to the status quo, not having increased finances.

What others had mimic or do what's expected of me lead me into body dysmorphic disorder, overeating and under eating, negative self-talk, compared myself to others, self-sabotage to the point I would talk myself out of not feeling qualified for a position. I didn't want others to speak highly of me and didn't want to be seen or have my accomplishments spoken of. I had a conversation with my life coach and discovered I neglect myself. I put others and things before my own needs. Causing me to show that I disliked myself. I did not admit it, but I showed it in my daily actions.

Psalm 139:14 reminds me that I am fearfully and wonderfully made. I must be intentional about self-care, positive self-talk, and balance life, daily. I've learned to say affirmations and speak the word of God to build self-confidence. I now have all the tools needed to be successful within.

Hypervigilance

My first time going to a secular concert I went to see my homeboy Joe at Aretha Franklin Amphitheatre, then it was called Chene Park in Detroit Michigan. I decided to wear a tube pants suit with a jacket. It was about 95 degrees. My friend talked about me so badly for having on a jacket. I was concerned about the church people seeing me with my arms and back out. I wore it most of the concert.

Let us not forget due to my hypervigilance I was also fearful that God was going to get me for going to the concert. Mercy Lord! I just enjoy his music as a musician. I took the jacket off but felt uncomfortable but felt cool. I will never forget walking to the car yelling to the sky I did not go to hell. No, not because I participated in the concert festivities. It was clean fun, yet I was hypervigilant. According to Merriam-Webster, hypervigilance is a state of being extremely alert to potential danger or threat.

I would have Hypervigilance drinking water in the church, standing in the pulpit, showing arms, falling short of God's will for my life, over analyzing not wanting to go to hell, mindful of others' expectations of me as a leader and more which caused me to have heightened levels of anxiety due to religious trauma. Lesson learned: relax and believe in your decision. Stop second guessing yourself. Allow God to have his way to calm you down and know that all is well.

Lack of Boundaries

"Sis. Mel, I need you here on time and ready to serve before service starts; ok, I replied." I would sacrifice going home to shower, eat, and get my daughter together to get to church on time to serve. It had gotten so bad that I had to call a meeting with my leaders to request a day off to meet my personal needs. They reported I could miss twice a month, but it took a few years to build up the courage to even ask them if I could get some time for personal activities such as laundry, cooking, and relaxing.

They controlled my dating life, who I hung out with and kept me in front of purity culture. However, I did not have enough strength to report to them that they were giving manipulation vibes. I experienced a lot of hurt reported as love. I continued to show strength, resilience, faithfulness and did all things unto the Lord and my leaders. Lesson learned: the bible reported Matthew 20: 3-4, "whatever is right he will pay." I did not see much harvest which caused me to question God and the religious system.

Make sure you have clear, honest, and respected boundaries for yourself. Always seek God for direction. My inability to say no was clothed in the scripture, Colossians 3:23, "Do it heartily, as to the Lord, and not unto men." I would often sing at concerts, weddings, funerals, services with groups and more anytime the request was made. I had to learn to create boundaries to avoid burning out.

Sexual Dysfunction

Sex is discussed in two ways in the church: abstinence for singles and bed undefiled for the married. Ok, who teaches and trains the engaged and or single ready to mingle. Sweet Jesus, there is no one I know that teaches the middle. Oh wait, I do. I recall talking to my sisters to prepare as needed and let the Lord help the rest of the way lol. I would not say that this is biblical but to educate yourself is helpful indeed. By the church emphasizing purity culture rightfully so biblically talking to other sisters causes struggle, shame, feeling dirty, increased desire or low desire causing dysfunction and sometimes being unprepared.

Lesson learned: to make sure you are knowledgeable and ready when God allow.

Mental Health Disorder

My religious trauma experience has caused me to experience post-traumatic stress disorder, depression, anxiety, obsessive-compulsive disorder, eating disorder and addictions. I did not know that I had these disorders until I journeyed through to healing from religious trauma. I started to examine my life to determine why I do certain things.

What came up for me was my lineage, bloodline with religion, experience, thoughts, emotions and how religion has caused trauma in my life causing me to have disorders, triggers, and stressors.

Finally

After reading about religious trauma on therapist.com I was able to connect to the article so much that I was able to see myself in all ten symptoms people can deal with in religious trauma. Religious trauma is real, and I know because I have completed research and have experienced it firsthand. The church in my past has been harmful, stressful, and degrading. I have seen many who suffer in silence and or don't acknowledge that they may have a few religious trauma symptoms due to the way others may feel about them expressing their true feelings. Please note that as well that could be connected to a symptom. When I found out this was an issue for me, I went on a journey to heal the church girl's wounded heart within me. I do not just want to heal. I would like to see others heal along with me from religious trauma. Others I know started to heal by really developing a relationship with God. Not with people, leaders, things etc. but with God. No more suffering in silence!

Healing your religious trauma today will have you on a clear path to doing what God says. It will have you in a place to forgive those who have hurt and the institution that harmed you creating boundaries and getting closer to God. I am here as a witness, if you do not deal with your religious trauma it will merge into your everyday task and follow you into every stage of your life. I had to get to a place of forgiveness and allow God to rebirth and create in me a clean heart and renew a right spirit within me.

It was not until one day that I was working with my life coach, and I was able to see that I was taking care of everyone else's needs but my own. Why did I behave the way that I did? I had to sit in my life journey within the religious community. I discovered many things. I learned some wonderful things that can never be erased, and some hurtful and harmful things as well. I just learned it is important to do your work and journey to healing to ensure freedom.

~ Prayer ~

Heavenly Father in the name of Jesus,

I come before You, carrying the wounds of past hurts caused by those who claimed to speak in Your name. I ask for Your healing touch to restore the parts of my heart that have been broken by pain, disappointment, and spiritual abuse.

Help me to release the burden of shame, guilt, and fear that have been placed upon me, and replace them with Your love, grace, and truth. Remind me of who You truly are a God of compassion, mercy, and kindness. Restore my faith in you, apart from the actions of those who have misrepresented your character.

Guide me on a path of healing, so I may find peace in Your presence and wholeness in my soul. Lead me to new understanding, clarity, and freedom in my relationship with You. Surround me with supportive, loving people who reflect Your true heart.

I trust you to mend what has been broken and lead me to a place of healing, strength, and victory. Thank you for your unfailing love and for the new beginning you offer. In Jesus name, Amen.

As you are reading these words allow them to rest in your heart and my prayer for you is that you will continue to seek God with all your heart, mind, soul, and strength continuing your path to freedom. May this prayer offer comfort and a sense of renewal as you journey toward healing your religious trauma.

Please answer the questions below:

Personal Experience

1. Can you describe your experience within your religious community?

2. Were there specific events or teachings that felt harmful or traumatic to you?

3. How has your relationship with your faith or spirituality changed over time?

Emotional and Psychological Impact

1. What emotions or thoughts arise when you think about your religious experiences?

2. Have you experienced feelings of guilt, shame, or fear related to your religious upbringing?

3. In what ways has religious trauma affected your mental health or sense of self?

Social and Community Effects

1. How have your relationships with family or community members, been impacted by your religious experiences?

2. Do you feel isolated or disconnected from those who remain in the religious community?

3. Have you sought support from others who have experienced similar religious trauma?

RELIGIOUS TRAUMA WORKSHEET

Step 1: Reflecting on Your Pain

1. Think about a time when you felt deeply hurt

o What happened during that time?

o Who was involved?

o How did it make you feel emotionally, spiritually, or physically?

2. Reflection:

Write a few sentences describing this experience!

_____

_____

_____

_____

Step 2: Naming Your Pain

2. Label the specific emotions or feelings you experienced.

Check all that apply or write in your own:

o Betrayal

o Anger

- o Guilt
- o Shame
- o Abandonment
- o Fear
- o Confusion
- o Loneliness
- o Grief
- o Rejection
- o Other: _____

Step 3: Exploring the Sources

3. **What do you believe caused these feelings?**

(Consider specific situations, relationships, or environments that contributed to this pain.)

Reflection:

List the factors or people that contributed to these emotions.

_____

_____

_____

Which of these sources are directly tied to religious or spiritual experiences?

_____

_____

_____

Example: A leader's hurtful actions, church teachings that felt oppressive, etc.

Reflection:

Identify specific spiritual or religious sources, if applicable.

Step 4: The Impact on You

How has this pain impacted your relationship with yourself, others, or your faith?

_____

_____

_____

_____

Reflection:

Write about how these experiences shaped your current worldview, behavior, or feelings.

_____

_____

_____

_____

Do you feel this pain is still influencing your decisions today?

Yes / No

If yes, in what ways?

_____

_____

_____

_____

Step 5: Healing Reflection

What would it look like to begin healing from these sources of pain?

(Consider small steps, like setting boundaries, seeking therapy, or talking to trusted individuals.)

Reflection:

List a few actions you could take to start the healing process.

_____

_____

_____

Step 6: Moving Forward

What positive lesson or strength can you take from this pain?

(Often, we gain resilience, compassion, or wisdom from our experiences, even if they were difficult.)

Reflection:

Write down any strengths or insights you have gained.

_____

_____

_____

Final Thought

Healing from emotional and spiritual pain takes time, but acknowledging the sources is a crucial first step. Use this worksheet as a tool for your healing journey, revisiting it as needed. You deserve peace, and each step you take toward identifying and addressing your pain brings you closer to wholeness.

At Radiant Diamond Enterprise LLC, we specialize in empowering women to transform their lives from trauma to triumph. Our coaching and consulting services are designed to guide women, especially those in the religious community, through a healing journey that leads to victory and personal growth. With a focus on emotional and spiritual well-being, we provide the tools and support needed to rebuild confidence and achieve lasting success. Join us on a path to becoming the radiant, victorious woman you were always meant to be."

Go to www.radiantdiamond.org to complete a religious trauma quiz for assistance. Phone: 248-531-8121

GRACE IN THE TRAUMA

Author Sofia Logan

How the hell did I get here? This has been such a reversal question in my life. I have asked myself this question in my valleys and even more so in my victories. "How the hell did I get here," can be a painful question but also a purposeful question. I have asked God, "how the hell did I get here" in reference to being in very low, unbearable places in my life and I have repeated that same question to God in seasons after experiencing his Glory when I felt I didn't deserve it. But can I tell you, life is a process.

Writing this book is a process, maturing into the woman God has called you and I to be is a process. I did not know that then, but I know now, we are all in a process to his promise. We sometimes do not get to choose our process, but we do get to choose to stay in the process until the promise is fulfilled. The Bible tells us "Endure like a good soldier," 2 Timothy 3-5 so it matters "HOW" we go through. I may not have always agreed with my processes but there has always been something in me that knew, better was coming. No matter what we go through it is important we never fix our minds on the process, or we will miss Gods promises. The enemy loves when we lose sight of God, so he entangled us in our process so much that we start to believe that's Gods plan for our lives (never fumble your process). It is our job to believe whatever God has promised us and it is God's job to deliver us every time.

Life has not always been beauty and rainbows for me, it was hard for me to even imagine I could be anything other than what I had been. My environment had shaped and molded the life I lived. Conditional upbringing can be a curse that we do not often realize is a curse because when it has a sense of normalcy, and it runs in your bloodline we often believe, "this is just how we are" and that is the very thing that creates generational curses.

My mother was addicted to crack cocaine, born a crack baby, dysfunctional childhood, father abandonment, childhood molestation, high school dropout, my own drug addiction, a teenage mother, and that is just to share the least. My chances of believing I could be anything different were tainted due to my upbringing and personal life choices. Trauma can either make you, or break you, it all depends on how you choose to tell your story. So today, I choose to tell my story from a place I have never shared from and that is from a whole place with broken memories.

As I had begun to write, the Lord told me, "Write with grace" such a profound word. So, I titled my story "Grace in the Trauma" because despite what has happened to me or who I feel has hurt me, I know God and that is the greatest victory after any trauma.

I was born October 10th, 1986, in Detroit, Michigan to my beautiful Black mother and my wealthy Arabic father. Yes, I am what the world would call "mixed." As we know Arabic men having babies with Black women was forbidden in the 1980's and even more so now. I first believed the spirit of rejection had been upon me since the time of conception. Which made me question my existence many times. I would think to myself, "if I was a mistake, why the hell am I here? Was I supposed to be born? Did my parents even love me? Why did they give me to my grandparents?" These are just a small fraction of the questions I asked myself before having a relationship with Christ. The Bible tells us in Jeremiah 29:11, "For I know the plans I have for you, plans to prosper you and not to harm you, plans to give you hope and a future. So can I remind you, you are not a mistake, and neither am I.

I grew up at a time when grandparents raised all their grandchildren. We grew up with our cousins being our siblings, sleeping with pallets on the living room floor, three of us sleeping in a small bunk bed, fire hydrants as our water parks, hot summer days, bike riding, BBQ's, Dazzy Dukes and uncle Luke music from, "2 Live Crew" those were the days. We used to have a ball coming up as kids, I come from a very silly dysfunctional family where being soft would get your feelings hurt. We could talk smack all day, piss each other off, argue but we were not allowed to fight one another.

My grandfather would kick our butts if we fought each other, after his passing I am not sure what the hell happened, but we'll get to that later. My grandmother was a very meek woman with the patience of Job and the heart of David. She was so loving and embracing as I think of her now. I am not sure how she did it BUT the strength of woman can never be measured when she is the pillar for her family. Despite the drug addictions the women in my family went through I was raised by very strong boisterous, dominant, powerful women. Who had a sense of humor but would kick your butt at the same time, our home was full of entertainment and excitement all the time.

My grandparents kept a very full busy home coming up as kids, it was like a revolving door at times. There was always a lot of activity going on in our home. Kids running in and out, our parents battling their drug addictions, people living with us who had nowhere to go, cousins living with us because their mother left them on the porch. My siblings and I lived there because our mother was in the height of her cocaine addiction, my aunts and uncle because they were in their addictions, I mean we saw a lot coming us as kids. Our environment was so chaotic, but we are taught to believe these things were normal or this is just how our family is and now as an adult I look back and I beg to differ.

Addictions were normal growing up as kids. From a kid to an adult, I have witnessed generations of addictions in my family. Additional curses are a spirit that runs in our blood line and have demolished the talents of my family. They became nothing more than addicts with a dream. Is everyone on drugs no, but very few are successful which is sad because we have such a gifted family whose potential has been robbed due to the spirit of addiction that has been latched on to our bloodline for centuries.

Anytime you have multiple people in your family battling the same addiction, that is a curse over your bloodline that can only be broken in the spirit. If the spirit is never broken it passes itself from generation to generation devouring one after another. Molestation is another spirit that has roots in our bloodline, this spirit is quiet and clever. It is deep rooted because it has never been confronted or exposed out of protection for the predator. Meanwhile the victims, including myself and many others in my family suffer from this abuse because Black families hide molestation. They fear embarrassment more than protecting a little girl's innocence.

There is this deep part of me that hates this happened to me and no one did anything about it. I am not sure if my resentment is due to what happened or what did not happen. My heart aches when I think about how so much of my childhood trauma was tucked under a rug and ignored. Was I not important enough for someone to fight for me? And when I mentioned I have been molested by my cousin multiple times, I was questioned as if I was lying. My family has a way to make you feel you are lying or wrong for exposing dark rooted secrets because the Lord has called you to be free. God will always raise someone up in your family to expose the spirits that has been keeping families in bondage. When people don't want to be free, or their guilt and shame won't allow them to be free, they will deem you as complicated or choose not to deal with you because you're exposing a spirit they have been attached to for years.

Typically, this is how families operate when they cannot hide anymore, and their years of secrets begin to be exposed. I remember being questioned by a family member about a podcast I did, and I remember they questioned me as if I were lying about the things I said. I responded and said, "you are not mad at me, you are mad because I told the truth. Where is the lie, I asked? I said to her, "Did I lie? She said "no" I said OK, so it was not because I lied, it is because I am exposing what has been hidden.

It may sound ugly and hard, but it is the truth and if y'all want to live a lie go ahead but God has called me to be free. Never let anyone make you feel your freedom is a crime as if you are doing wrong for calling out what has happened to you. This is why so many of us have hidden trauma. We will not talk about what has happened because people will make you feel guilty for healing.

It has taken me a long time to be confident in my ability to speak on the way I feel about the things that have happened to me. We have been taught to let things go. Keep quiet because that is your mother or that is going to start a big mess. They don't want to deal with that right now or you are viewed as an issue for speaking up. Silence is wise but it is also a prison many of us have been locked up in for years.

We fear speaking because we do not want to get someone else in trouble. The world has surely messed us up. We are loyal to the Criminal and disloyal to our freedom. In the interrogation room you have a choice to speak and be free or keep quiet and serve someone else's time. The choice is yours and society has taught us to imprison ourselves while the criminal is free and those days for me are long over. My voice is my identity, and it has become my sound of freedom. I pray the same for you as you are reading this book. I pray you find your voice in a world that is so loud and boisterous that you do not hide in the crowd that you will come out and be heard because someone, somewhere needs your story.

I thought nothing much of my story at first because remember I thought it was normal. I thought well this is how I was raised or this how we are. It was not until I went through my seven-year drug addiction that I realized, hey wait this is not ok. This is not normal for someone in their twenties to be entering rehab due to a drug addiction. I spent my twenties as a drug addict, how hurtful is that? We must stop normalizing addictions in our families, it truly messes our family members up. Get them help, set up an intervention, try to encourage them as much as possible to get clean and live a healthy life.

Please do not allow your family, if possible, to live in a place that is slowly killing them, I speak for all addicts that has been bound by a substance. There is hope and there is freedom, and you too can be clean and live an abundant life. If God did it for me, He surely will do it for you. There are many resources available that will help you get and stay clean as you journey through your sobriety. You can always access resources by calling the number on the back of your insurance cards. That includes state insurance, HMO, PPO, EPO etc., they all have resources for addictions and remember "Recovery is not about perfection, it's about progression." Take it one day at a time and do what is best in each day, make the best choice in that day as it will get you to tomorrow.

My addiction stemmed from a variety of trauma but also from a bloodline curse. By the time I was 21 years old I addicted to Opioids. I started with just having cramps one day and went to my cousin for something for pain and she gave me a Vicodin and the moment it kicked in; my spirit fell in love with the feeling. It started with just one or two a day and increased to where I was taking three and four at one time but numerous times a day.

Vicodin was the start of my addiction. By my second year in, I was addicted to many other prescription medications. Which caused me to start lying, stealing from my place of employment, selling drugs, getting others hooked. I am not proud of this at all, and it hurts me to even share this, but the story must be told. I was getting so bad I start stealing needles and Toradol injecting myself for a quicker high. I had done all this about five times until I was pulled over by the police and they found the medication and needles in my glove box of my car. I have never shared this part of my story until now, there is a season for everything. I have always been really embarrassed by it so I always hid it but remember God cannot heal what we will not reveal. I am so thankful to God because I could have really done some serious jail time if I were ever charged for the things I have done. But his grace was so sufficient in my life during that time, and I did not even know it.

By the time I was 27 years old I admitted myself into residential rehab. Which means I had to complete detox and release for about 3 days and 27 days in an inpatient treatment program. My first night there I shook out so badly because my body was detoxing which caused me to need immediate medical attention. Those nurses came rushing to me, it was the first time in life I thought, "how the hell will I survive this?" I felt like death or at least that is what that experience

was like. I went through days of nausea, diarrhea, anxiety, depression, fatigue, chills, sweats, and excessive sleeping. I made it through all of that as a 27-year-old young mother whose son had to be left behind for a while so I could get clean.

I was so young and innocent I did not know much about life or being a parent but what I did know is I did not want my son to experience the life I had. I did not want to do what my mother had done with me to my son and that is give me away because she was unable to care for me properly because of her drug addiction. See how generations repeat itself when the spirit of the issue is not broken, it carries over to the next generation.

This is why getting clean and maintaining my sobriety has been a priority for me. I know now that I broke a generational curse in my bloodline even if that is just for my children. Would I love to see my whole family free, absolutely. I pray for deliverance and freedom all the time, but I know that is a stronghold that only God can break. My job is to continuously pray. The reason I have been so adamant about maintaining my sobriety is because I never want the spirit of addiction to fall on my son. It is my job to stay clean so that I can give him a fair chance at life, his freedom is predicated on my deliverance.

I had my son at the age of 18 years old, I did not know how to be a mother or what a healthy mother looked like, but I knew I wanted to be something and someone different from what I had encountered growing up. I met his dad when I was just 16 years old at the time he was twenty-one and I knew nothing about being with a man that old. I was so young, misguided and easily manipulated.

I was searching for a love that no one could give me but God. I wish I had known that God loved me. It would have saved me from a lot of decisions I have made or abuse I allowed. Love is so important to display to your daughters as they are growing up. It will keep them out of the hands of loving the wrong man. Love is so powerful, and it covers a multitude of issues depending on how you display love.

My interpretation of love was so miscommunicated to me growing up. I saw abuse and dysfunction connected to love. I grew up thinking love was violence and addiction, and this is why I allowed myself at 16 until I was nineteen to go through domestic violence and became an addict at 21 because my drug also became my love. My son's father was a wolf in sheep clothing. his is when someone appears to be good but is evil or deceitful. I hated him for years for the way he treated me for all the abuse, lies, manipulation, baby mama drama, cheating, and outside children I had to find out about, I mean the list goes on.

The man was a menace and was very clever in how he would manipulate others to believe he was this innocent person, and I had the problem. I did not know any better and I started believing I had a problem, or I was the problem. I mean this man messed my mind up so bad that I allowed him to abuse me because I thought he had reason. Now what kind of mess is that he had me gone out my mind. I was so insecure and scared at all at the same time and I carried that spirit around with me for many years.

The Lord finally broke that thing this year (2024). This man made me scared of him, he got off on knowing I feared him. He was pure evil. I remember him jumping on me one day and he put his cigarette out on me as I was lying on the floor pregnant with my son. I recall another time driving in my car and he wanted to take me home so he can use my car and do God knows what. He bit my fingers so badly trying to take my car keys that I still have the teeth marks on my fingers till this day and this happened 20 years ago.

It was not until my son was born; I began to fight him back. I was tired of them ass whooping's. I had finally had enough because I knew no one was coming for me and I had to stand up for myself. I did not want my son seeing me being abused and I did not want my son growing up thinking it was ok to abuse a woman. I had to fight back, I had no choice, my life depended on it, and I was finally tired. I remember him saying to me, "I will stop fighting you when you learn to fight back" well I did. The first time I ever really fought him back was upstairs in my bedroom and my son was in his car seat and he was trying to snatch the car seat so he could take my son.

He happened to bend down and out of me came a rage I never had. I took the stereo system off the dresser and slammed it on his head and back. All I know is he was not taking my son. I may have never fought for me, but I be damn I did not fight for my son. You mess with my son you wake up another beast in me. I am so protective over my son always has been and always will be. My son didn't ask to come into the world, so it is my job to make sure he's safe at all times. I believe God used my son to make me tougher because I was not about that life prior to my son being born but domestic violence can make you violent.

I went through a season where I was not taking mess from anyone. I was always guarded and ready to fight, and I was overly defensive. But can I just tell you God is a healer, a redeemer, and a restorer. I have watched God change my life and where I was once angry, I now have peace. Where I was once violent, I now have victory. I now realize that everything I have been through the Lord has delivered and protected me every time.

Can I remind you that God loves you and if he did it for me you are next on his list. If you are in a season of feeling overly stimulated when challenges arise, I need you to remember this scripture before you respond, "Do not be anxious about anything, but in everything by prayer and supplication with thanksgiving let your requests be made known to God" (Philippians 4:6). This scripture confirms God has your back because HEAVEN RESPONDS WHEN YOU'RE IN TROUBLE. Allow God to fight your battles. You will never be able to do what God can do. So, friends live in your peace and let nothing, and no one rob you of that.

I am not saying be a door mat, always stand up for you and never allow a man to put his hands on you. What I am saying think before you respond and allow God to fight your battles. Since my relationship with my son's father, I have never encountered physical abuse again and I am so thankful to God because I am not sure what the outcome would be. I pray the Lord knows what is best for me. My final straw with my son's father was one night I was sleep and he began jumping on me in my sleep.

I woke up to being punched in my face, choked, smothered with a pillow and my shirt being ripped. I was trying to get away and finally, made it down the stairs to my grandmother (Lord rest her precious soul) and he held my son by one arm on the steps and threw him across the hall to my grandmother's room. My son landed on the bed, thank God!!! I remember my grandmother saying, "I know you didn't throw this baby" and he looked me in my face and said, "now you can tell people I whooped your ass!" He left out that front door and I never went back.

When I looked in that mirror my face was so swollen it shifted to the whole right side of my face. My lips were busted, I had a huge knot on my forehead, scratches and marks over my neck and bruised eye. I mean he did exactly what he said, "whooped my ass." I am not sure what hurt me the most, him throwing my baby or the fear in my grandmother's face when I looked at her. Every time I replayed that moment in my mind, I saw her face and I never wanted to see her fearful again off something or someone I allowed in our home. I was done and I never looked back. I moved from my grandmother's home because I knew he would look for me there and I moved to the suburbs with my mother and her husband. For months I broke all lines of communication and whereabouts. I was finally free and released from my enemy. Always remember this when the Lord finally releases you from whatever is hurting you, do not return!!!!

As you can see, I've had my good days, I've had my hills to climb. I have had my weary day and some sleepless nights but when I look around and I think things over all my good days outweigh my bad days and I will not complain. God has been good to me better than this whole world could ever be, God has been my redeemer and restorer. I love that song; it ministers to me every time. Something's I may not ever understand why I had to go through them but what always keep me sane is knowing God has a plan for me and His plans for me is to prosper me and not harm me, give me hope and a future (Jeremiah 29:11).

He brings and has brought me out every time. Even as a 7-year-old kid not knowing or understanding why my 11-year-old sister Monnalisa was called home at such an early age always has been questionable. I was so devastated as a kid, and I was left to cope with my sister's death on my own. At just 7 years old I was so torn. I do not recall anyone asking if I was ok or how I was holding up after she passed.

I failed the second grade because of her death. I was so sad after she passed. She was the closest thing I ever had to a mother. She used to get me ready for school, comb my hair and wash my underclothes out in the sink and hang them to dry so I could have clothes for school. She was my protector, and I know if she were alive, I would not have gone through the things I went through.

She was left to care for me because our mother was addicted to crack cocaine. My sister and I were raised by our grandparents. Our older siblings had moved out and we were the only two left and after she passed. I had no one from my mother's womb left in the home where I was raised. So, my cousin became siblings and aunts became my mother, everyone became what I did not have.

My sister was hit by a car and ran over in front of my grandparents' home. Her and my aunt were playing around in the house and my sister was standing in a chair putting a light bulb in and my aunt came passed and hit her on the butt and my sister chased her out the house and my aunt ran across the street and my sister never made it across.

The car hit my sister so hard that she flew feet into the air and landed on her head right near my grandfather's car. When we all ran outside, she was inches from being underneath the car with blood everywhere running from her face and head. I remember this so vividly and I was just 7 years old. This was something my family had never been through. It was difficult for everyone at that time and her death sent our mother to an even deeper depression and addiction. It was the only coping mechanism she knew. I cannot blame her; she did what she knew to do. I cannot imagine how my mother felt and honestly, I never want to know.

The most shocking thing about my sister's death is she did not die from the hit and run; she passed away from the negligence of the hospital. Which I am limited to express due to lawful reasons. However, my siblings and I have endured many obstacles and life altering experiences which caused us great pain, but God has kept us through everyone.

My siblings and I all have a story, and we all share and express our stories differently because we all endured different situations and had different outcomes, but can I tell you all my mother kids are blessed. My mother may have been through hell and back, but my mother's womb is blessed. The Lord sure has a way of rewarding you in the end. So, to anyone that may not seem to understand what you are going through or why you are going through it remember this, the weapon may form but it will not prosper.

You will have victory every time, you will prosper in every way, and nothing is by accident. That even though he slay you, yet shall you trust Him. Maintain your ways before Him. (Job 13:15) so it is not about what you go through, it is how you go through it. It is God's job to bring you out, it is your job to trust that He will do just that.

As I have shared just a snippet of my story, I pray you find peace after your trauma or even during your trauma. I pray that your faith does not fail because people fail you. My prayer is that you encounter God, the only true living God. I pray you heal and make it your priority. Healing is a choice and can often feel unfair when you are left to do the work, but I promise it is your responsibility to take care of you. I pray you forgive and release the people that have hurt you and I pray they release you so you can walk in total freedom. I pray your heart remains soft after hard and unbearable times. May your mind find peace the peace that God promises us "I am leaving you with a gift - a peace of mind and heart" John 14:27.

May your mind become a resting place for restoration. I pray you experience a healed life. Healing is a journey that only you can go through. I want that for you. Healing brings a wholeness to your life, so I pray that the Lord take every broken piece and create a "Masterpiece." Your brokenness has meaning and it defines where you once were so never be ashamed of your journey, it has your destiny connected to it.

This journey is not easy, but it is so worth it. I know you may ask God all the time, Lord help, lord why, or lord please heal me, but can I tell you God is creating something so beautifully inside of you. I know that may seem hard to

believe here is a reminder, "The Lord is close to the brokenhearted and save those who are crushed in spirit, it takes time for heart wounds to heal" (Psalm 34:18). Be patient with yourself and allow God to heal you with time.

Lastly, be resilient and recover from every attack, every lie, every childhood trauma, and every adult life experience, which has caused you to doubt yourself. That has caused you to plant seeds to make you believe you are not good enough. As a matter of fact, believe that you are more than enough. The Bible says, "We are fearfully and wonderfully made, created in his image" (Psalm 139:14). So, know who you are in God, not your trauma. Do not allow your pain to create your image.

Healing creates a new identity. The person you see when you are broken will not be the same person you see when you heal. This is why it is important to surround yourself with healed people because broken people, hurt people but healed people heal people. Change your circle and watch God change your life. I am truly happy for you and the woman you will become, once you heal you will thrive and encounter women you can help heal. We all have a story we just must heal to tell it.

I hope you have enjoyed yourself here but before I close allow me to end with this. I now have a high school diploma, two associate's degrees, finishing my bachelor's degree now at Wayne State, I was accepted into Wayne State Psychology program this past fall.

I have obtained many certificates and certifications along the way. I serve as an Evangelist in and outside the church, I love drawing souls to Christ. I am recently engaged and will be welcoming my new husband to be this winter. My son graduated high school last year and pursuing his career as a chef and I have countless blessings and miracles of what the Lord has done for me and my family. I wanted to share this with you so you know if He did it for me, God will surely do it for you. Roman's 8:28, "For we know that all things work TOGETHER for good to those who LOVE God, who are called according to his purpose."

I want you to take a moment and reflect and ask yourself these questions?

Where are you in your healing process?

_____

_____

_____

_____

_____

What are you holding on to that keeps you from healing?

_____

_____

_____

_____

_____

Do you have a personal relationship with God?

_____

_____

_____

What are you doing to heal?

_____

_____

_____

_____

Have you truly forgiven who hurt you?

_____

_____

_____

_____

_____

I had to answer these questions before, and I remember
crying writing the answers but as I released God restored.
Never feel weak for crying or expressing your feelings about
what has hurt you. You are strong when you let hurt go, not
when you keep it in. Crying is cleansing and only strong
people encounter this level of deliverance. Do not allow this
world to make you feel ashamed for healing. Society has
conditioned us to believe we have to be hard and strong all
the time and that is not true. Society will have you live in

your trauma and never heal because we care too much about what others think. Can I please encourage you to get away from those people and find you a community that will help you heal.

Prayer

Let us pray: Father God, in the name of Jesus I thank you, that I am not my trauma. Lord, I thank you for making all things new. Lord, I thank you now for a renewed mindset and a reset to go forth in what you have called me to do. Lord, thank you that I am no longer bound, and I have been released by the hands and hearts of my abusers and I have released them to you for judgement. Lord, I will no longer hold anyone hostage in my heart. Lord, I am free and to use it wisely to make your name great. So, father, heal me as only you can and spring forth my new identity as I embrace a healed place. Lord, release comfort where I am hurting and peace where I am battling. Settle my spirit by knowing you have my back. God, if you are for me who can be against me. I thank you now for your strength, which is made perfect in my weakness. I could not have survived it without you. You are the GREAT I AM! and for that God, I AM!!!!! It is in Jesus' name I pray AMEN!!!!!

I am always an available for an email to communicate "SofiaLoganMinistries@yahoo.com" I would love to hear your story and help you navigate through your process.

Thank you!

Sofia Lorraine Logan

"Sofia Logan Ministries"

<u>A Declaration to Forgive</u>

On this Day _____I _____,

Declare to Forgive, _____

I forgive you for_____

_____

_____

_____

_____

_____

_____

_____

_____

_____

_____

_____

_____

I am writing this letter, not because I excuse or condone the offense. There are things I will never fully understand, and I may never receive the apology that I once hoped for. You and the incident will no longer hold me hostage. I choose to forgive. I choose to release the anger, embarrassment, hurt and resentment that I have carried for too long. What you did caused me so much pain. I questioned myself, my existence and my worth. I felt so much weight and bondage from carrying it. It's no longer mine to carry. I forgive because peace belongs to me. I forgive because joy belongs to me. I forgive you because I have been forgiven. I release you into the past to make room for my own healing.

May Gods peace be with you and may God show you mercy.

Signed,

Who is Michelle? I am a trauma survivor and now an educator. I am healed from my trauma. As it was stated in the book, "you can't heal, without the healer." Although I was considered just average and did not do well in school as a child, I now hold two degrees and am the author of over 20 books. I would not be here if it were not for Gods grace!

Thank you taking the time to read, Inside these Walls. It is my prayer that you can look inside your own walls, figure out what is weighing you down and find the strength to heal from it. Know that healing is yours! My final thought to you is that trauma does not have to win!

I can be contacted at generationssoar@gmail.com